Magic Ballerina™

Rosa and the Secret Princess

Darcey Bussell

HarperCollins *Children's Books*

*To Phoebe and Zoe, as they are the inspiration
behind Magic Ballerina.*

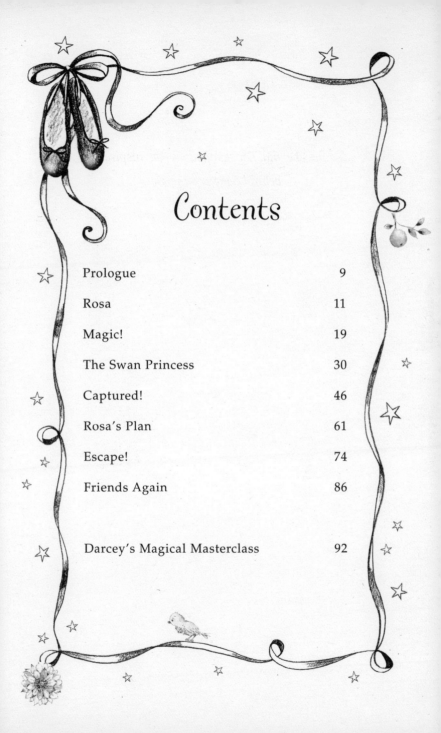

Contents

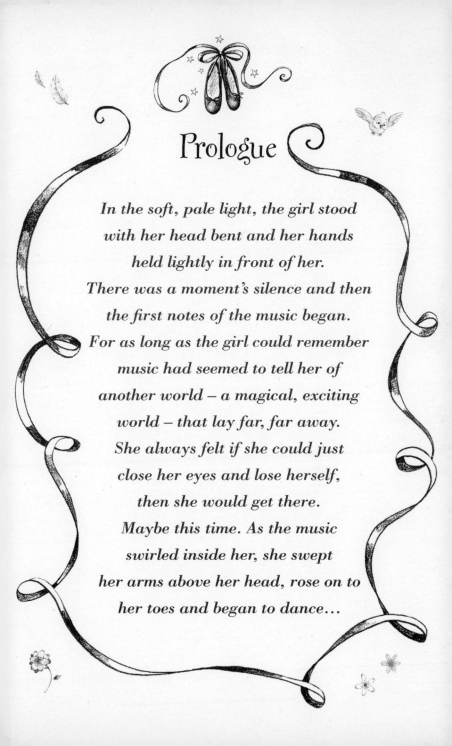

Prologue

*In the soft, pale light, the girl stood
with her head bent and her hands
held lightly in front of her.
There was a moment's silence and then
the first notes of the music began.
For as long as the girl could remember
music had seemed to tell her of
another world – a magical, exciting
world – that lay far, far away.
She always felt if she could just
close her eyes and lose herself,
then she would get there.
Maybe this time. As the music
swirled inside her, she swept
her arms above her head, rose on to
her toes and began to dance…*

Rosa

Rosa ran up the steps to the old front door and turned the brass handle. She liked to get to Madame Za-Za's ballet school early so she could warm up before class and today was particularly special because it was her first day back after the summer holidays. She couldn't wait for classes to start again.

Hurrying to the changing rooms, she put on her pink leotard. Over the summer she had made a new friend, Olivia, who was going to be starting at the ballet school that very day. Rosa had arranged to meet her before class to show her around. She was really looking forward to it!

It's going to be very different this term, she thought. Several of the older girls who had been in her class had moved up into another group. Rosa was going to miss them, particularly her friend, Delphie. At the end of last term, Delphie had given Rosa a pair of red ballet shoes that didn't fit her any longer. They were very old and the leather was very soft. Now Rosa took them out of her bag and put them on, crossing the ribbons neatly over

her ankles and tying
them firmly. They
fitted perfectly.
When Delphie
had given her
the shoes, she
had said
something odd –
something about:
"Watch out for King Rat".
Rosa didn't have a clue what she had meant
by that, and the few times she had seen
Delphie in the summer, the dark-haired girl
had refused to tell her. She had just kept
smiling mysteriously and saying that the
ballet shoes were very special.

And indeed, Rosa loved them and couldn't

wait to start dancing. Going over to the
mirror, she fixed her long white-blonde hair
into a bun. Then she put on her favourite
hairclip before leaving the changing rooms
to go to the ballet studio. She wished she
could come to classes every day. *When I'm
older I will,* she thought. She was determined
she was going to be a ballerina just like her
mum had once been. Her mother didn't
dance any more because she had been in a
car accident, which had left her in a
wheelchair, but she helped Rosa practise.

Rosa went to the long wooden *barre* that
ran all the way around the walls and began
to warm up. The red ballet shoes felt really
comfortable, and it was so lovely to be back
in the ballet studio again that she completely

lost track of the time. A little while later she looked at the clock and gasped. It was only a few minutes until the class started. She had promised Olivia she would meet her in the changing rooms almost ten minutes ago!

As Rosa ran back to the changing rooms, she was worried that Olivia would be alone and upset. She burst through the changing room doors and stopped dead…

Olivia was standing there with two of the other girls from the class. She was laughing as one of them helped her tie her brown hair back and smiled, in what seemed to Rosa a casual way. "Oh, hi there, Rosa!"

"Hi. I'm… I'm sorry I wasn't here to meet you," Rosa said, feeling a bit silly to have burst in so quickly. She felt suddenly unsure of herself, seeing her friend so at ease.

Olivia smiled. "Don't worry. Everyone's been really friendly. Asha and Rebecca showed me round."

Asha, who was fixing Olivia's hair, smiled.

"Madame Za-Za's a cool teacher. I bet you're going to love coming to classes here, Olivia."

A mixture of emotions swirled around inside Rosa. She was pleased that Olivia wasn't upset but she also felt a tiny twinge of jealousy that the other girls had been the ones to take her new friend around. "I was going to show you how it worked and help you get ready," she said. She knew she sounded cross and grumpy but she couldn't stop herself. Olivia looked surprised. "But you weren't here, Rosa and…" She broke off. "Look, why don't you show me round again after class?"

"Oh, what's the point?" Rosa said angrily. "You've seen everything now!" And with that, she marched back to the ballet studio.

Magic!

As soon as Rosa got to the studio, her anger faded. She felt awful. She shouldn't have snapped like that. All Olivia had done was make friends with the others.

I'd better say sorry, Rosa thought guiltily. She felt annoyed with herself. Her mum was always telling her she needed to control her temper and think more before she acted but sometimes she just couldn't help herself. It just welled up inside her and came out – like all the times in her old school when the girls had teased her about her mum. Just then, Olivia came into the studio with the other girls and gave her a hurt look. But before Rosa could run over and apologise, Madame Za-Za also came in. The ballet teacher was wearing a calf-length dress and bangles on her wrists. Her hair was tied back in a loose bun. Her face was lined but her eyes were very bright. She clapped her hands for silence.

"Welcome, girls. Let's start at the *barre*. No talking please!"

Rosa knew there would be no chance to say sorry now until the end of the class. Madame Za-Za got very cross if she thought anyone was chatting and not listening.

"Facing the *barre*, first position please."

Rosa followed Madame Za-Za's instructions wishing she could apologise.

After they had worked at the *barre* and then in the centre of the room, Madame Za-Za told them that they were going to learn a dance from *Swan Lake*.

"Who can tell me the story of *Swan Lake*?" she asked.

Rosa put up her hand. It had been the last ballet her mother had ever danced in and one of her favourites. "It's about a magician who enchants a princess called Odette. In the

day time she's a swan – the Swan Queen –
but at night time she turns back into a girl."

"Very good," said Madame Za-Za. "That is
indeed the basis of the story. One night, a
prince sees the Swan Queen, falls in love
with her and invites her to a ball. But the evil
magician stops Odette from going and
instead uses magic to disguise his daughter,
Odile, to look like her. The prince thinking
Odile is Odette asks her to marry him."

Madame Za-Za smiled. "You will all be
swans dancing with the Swan Queen. Rosa, I
would like you to be the main part."

Rosa gasped. "Me!"

Madame Za-Za smiled at her. "I am sure
you will dance it very well."

Rosa was delighted. She listened intently

22

to Madame Za-Za's instructions as all
the swans surrounded the Swan Queen.

There was one tricky bit where she had to
dance to one side and then the other, before
turning another pirouette while the others
danced in towards her and then out, over
and over again. They practised it quite a few

times without the music and then Madame
Za-Za put the CD on. Rosa really wanted to
get it right. But she overbalanced on her
pirouette and bumped into Olivia, treading
heavily on her foot. Olivia gasped and
stumbled into Asha, knocking her over.

Madame Za-Za snapped the music off. "Honestly, girls. Come along, you can do better than that! Up you get, Asha. Let's try again."

Rosa looked quickly at Olivia. She tried to mouth "sorry" but Olivia turned away. Rosa groaned inwardly. She was sure Olivia thought she had stood on her foot on purpose.

When the class finished, she hurried towards her friend.

"Rosa!" Madame Za-Za called. "May I have a word please?"

Rosa shot a look at Olivia's disappearing back but there was nothing she could do. She walked back to the teacher. Madame Za-Za was putting away the CD. Rosa waited as she finished.

"I see you have the red ballet shoes, Rosa," Madame Za-Za said.

Rosa nodded. "Delphie Durand gave them to me."

Madame Za-Za smiled. "So they found the perfect home. Did you know they used to belong to me a long time ago?"

"No," Rosa said, in her astonishment forgetting about Olivia.

Madame Za-Za nodded. "They are very special shoes, Rosa."

"Delphie told me that," Rosa said.

"I hope you find out quite how special they are," Madame Za-Za smiled warmly. "Now, go and get changed."

Part of Rosa wanted to ask Madame Za-Za what she meant about the shoes being special but she also wanted to catch Olivia before she left. She hurried out but saw it was too late. Olivia was just going through the front door with her mother.

"Olivia!" Rosa called.

But Olivia had already walked out and the door was shutting behind her.

Rosa's heart sank. *I'll phone her and say sorry as soon as I get home,* she thought as she went to the changing room.

The other girls were just leaving. They

called goodbye and soon Rosa was on her own. She sat down and bent over to untie the ribbons on her red shoes. As she did so her feet started to tingle. She gasped. The shoes were sparkling and glowing!

She jumped to her feet and then cried out in astonishment as a swirl of rainbow colours and a sweet tinkling of music surrounded her. She started to spin round!

What was going on? She shut her eyes tightly, her heart pounding. Round and round she went until her feet met solid ground. She blinked.

She wasn't in the changing rooms any more, she was standing in a forest, and through the trees she could see a shimmering dark lake with a single swan swimming on it!

The Swan Princess

Rosa stared. Where was she? No wonder Delphie and Madame Za-Za had been telling her the ballet shoes were special! *They're magic*, she thought, her heart flipping. *Oh wow!*

There were tall trees all around her and to the right of the lake she could see a big, dark castle. What should she do? She couldn't just

stay standing there. Which way should she go?

Not to the castle, she decided. It looked so forbidding. Instead, she made her way cautiously through the trees towards the lake.

Suddenly, she saw a flash of pink ahead of her. There was someone dancing in the trees. She hurried forward and stopped in amazement as she saw that the dancer was a fairy! The fairy had a tutu made of layers of brown and pink silk and a pale pink bodice with sequins embroidered over it. Her wavy chestnut hair was tied back in a bun. She had delicate wings and in one hand she held a wand. As she saw Rosa, she stopped with a gasp. Her gaze flew to Rosa's feet. "You're

the girl with the red shoes! The new girl!"
She ran over, her brown eyes shining with
excitement. "Oh, I'm so glad to see you!"

"You are?" Rosa said in bewilderment.

"Of course!" The fairy seized her hands.
"You're here to help, aren't you? Sugar told
me you would come."

"Help?" echoed Rosa. "Who's Sugar? And where exactly am I?"

"You're in Enchantia, of course!" said the fairy breathlessly. "The magical land of ballet. Oh dear, I'm sorry," she said, looking at Rosa's bewildered face. "Sugar said you wouldn't have been here before and that I had to tell you everything from the beginning. It's just I'm so excited to see you. I haven't been doing proper magic for very long and I've never met a human before!"

Rosa smiled cautiously as the fairy's words tumbled out one after another. "So who exactly is Sugar?" she asked.

The fairy took a deep breath and spoke a little more slowly. "She's my older sister – the Sugar Plum Fairy - she knows lots about

magic. I'm Nutmeg by the way. Whenever
we have a big problem in Enchantia the red
ballet shoes bring someone from your world
who can help us, a girl who loves to dance."

Rosa stared at her.
So she was in a magic
land and she was
there to help!
"Will… will I get to
go home again?" she
asked.

Nutmeg nodded. "Of course. The shoes
will take you back when the problem is
solved. No time passes in the human world
while you're here so no one will even know
you've been gone."

Rosa breathed a sigh of relief. For a

moment she had thought about her mum waiting for her and getting really worried. That would have been dreadful!

"What's your name?" the fairy asked.

"Rosa."

"It's so lovely to see you, Rosa. We really need your help," Nutmeg said. "King Rat's causing dreadful trouble again!"

"King Rat!" Rosa breathed, remembering Delphie's words. So *that* must have been what Delphie was talking about. She must have come here too!

"Yes," replied Nutmeg. "You see everyone in Enchantia loves dancing except for that horrible rodent. He keeps coming up with mean plans to stop us and now he's taken the King and Queen's niece, Princess Cressida."

"Princess Cressida?" Rosa scratched her head. It was all a lot to take in.

"Yes, Cressida was on her way to visit her aunt and uncle to keep them company whilst their own daughter, Aurelia, is away. Nutmeg explained. Anyway, King Rat has captured Cressida to stop all the balls and dancing that would go on for her visit. Without her at the palace there won't be any celebrations."

"So where has he taken her?" breathed Rosa.

"She's here in his castle grounds," said Nutmeg. "He's put a spell on her so that by day she's a swan, but by night she's the princess again."

"Just like *Swan Lake*!" Rosa said excitedly.

"Yes, exactly," Nutmeg nodded. "That's where King Rat got the idea from. Look, there's Princess Cressida on the Enchanted Lake now." Nutmeg pointed towards the graceful white swan on the shimmering water. "Sugar has asked me to stand guard to check that King Rat doesn't whisk her away somewhere else or put even more spells on

her, but she doesn't even realise I'm here. You see she forgets all about being a princess in the day. It just comes back to her as the

sun sets and she flies back to her room in the castle's towers and turns back into her old self."

"Oh, the poor thing," Rosa said, her heart going out to the princess.

Nutmeg shivered. "Everyone in Enchantia keeps trying to think up a plan to rescue her, but we haven't come up with anything yet. If only we could get her out of King Rat's castle grounds, the enchantment would be broken. But the lake is enchanted so we can't swim

or row across to get her and she wouldn't recognise us anyway."

Rosa thought for a moment. "Can't you use magic to rescue her at night when she's locked inside?"

Nutmeg shook her head. "King Rat's magic is much too powerful. He's put spells on the castle so that no one else can do strong magic either in it or its grounds. I stay in the trees because some of my magic still works in the forest. Also, I can keep watch on Cressida and magic myself away if his horrible scary guards come." She clasped her hands together. "Oh, Rosa. Can *you* think of a way we could rescue the princess?"

Rosa stared at her helplessly and gulped. It all seemed pretty impossible. "I wish I could," she said. "But I really haven't got any other ideas."

"Then Princess Cressida will just have to stay a secret princess forever!" exclaimed Nutmeg, her eyes filling with tears.

"Look, we can't give up that easily!" Rosa declared. "Hmm, what could we do?" She glanced around. "You know, maybe we don't need magic to get us into the castle. Maybe we could just sneak inside. We could hide somewhere until the princess comes back then let her out of her room and all escape together!"

"But that would be really dangerous!" said Nutmeg. "King Rat's guards are very fierce!" She caught her breath. "Here they come now!"

A group of ten mice came swaggering around the side of the castle. Rosa stared. They were walking on their back legs and were way taller than her, with pointed teeth and long swords hanging from their belts.

They stopped. A couple of them leaned against the castle walls, the others mooched  about. They looked fed up.

"I'm bored of marching round the castle," one of them grumbled.

"Me too," said another. "My paws are hurting. King Rat's out at the moment so why don't we go and have a sit down?"

"Yeah!" said the first mouse. "If we go round to the other side of the castle we can listen out for King Rat coming back and when he gets here just start marching again." He looked around at the others. "What do you reckon?"

They all nodded. "Good plan!"

"What about the Sergeant?" said one. "If he sees us he'll go mad."

The first mouse shrugged. "He's inside somewhere. Probably in the kitchens stuffing his face. I bet he'll never notice. Come on!"

They all ambled off around the side of the castle.

Nutmeg shivered. "They're horrible!"

But Rosa's mind was racing with what the

mice had just said. "Did you hear what they were talking about? King Rat's out and they are going to take a break. Oh, Nutmeg! Why don't we try to get into the castle right now?"

"But it's daytime and Cressida is on the lake."

"So? We can hide somewhere inside until the sun sets and she comes back. It's the perfect opportunity. Come on! Let's see if there's a door or window open."

Rosa started to hurry through the trees towards the castle.

"Wait, Rosa!" exclaimed Nutmeg, flying after her. "It's too dangerous! The guards might change their minds and come back."

"Then we'd better be as quick as possible," said Rosa. "It's now or never!"

"No! I don't think we should," Nutmeg insisted. "Look, let's just stay here for a little while longer and see if we can think of another plan. Come on! I'm going back to the lake."

She flew back towards the lake. Rosa hesitated. She thought of the poor secret princess. She *had* to help her! Surely getting into the castle was the only way and while the guards were taking a break it was the

perfect opportunity! *I'm going to try and get in whether Nutmeg wants to come or not,* she decided impulsively. And she began to hurry through the trees.

Captured!

Rosa's eyes scanned the castle, but the only windows that were open were right up at the top of the tower. There was a small door to the right of the main entrance. Maybe that would be unlocked?

A short stretch of grass separated the wood and the castle. She took a deep breath and ran across it. Reaching the small door, she turned the handle… locked! Suddenly she heard a sharp voice from around the side of the castle…

"I can't believe you lot. Get back to patrolling the castle right now! Lying around! Lazing about! Honestly. I can't trust you for a second! If King Rat catches you he'll have your guts for garters. Come on! Hup two, hup two!"

There was the sound of general mumbling and grumbling and the stamp of boots heading towards the front of the castle.

Rosa froze to the spot. The guards were coming! She looked round desperately. Where could she hide? There were some giant pots that looked like they had once had plants in them.

Rosa raced to the nearest one and scrambled inside. The bottom was covered with old dry soil and as she landed, it blew up in clouds around her. She could feel a sneeze tickling in her nose…

She covered her face with her hands as the grumbling guards came around the side of

the building. Rosa could hear them passing near the plant pot and felt the sneeze building. She pinched her nose but she couldn't stop it!

"A… a… ACHOO!"

"What was that?" the leader's voice snapped out.

The guards' footsteps stopped.

"There's someone hiding!" said the
Sergeant. "Find them!"

Rosa huddled down in the bottom of the
plant pot, her heart beating painfully against
her ribcage. *Please don't look in here*, she
thought as footsteps echoed around her...

Too late... A pointed face peered over the
edge of the plant pot before shrieking out
loudly. "Oi, Sarge! I've found someone! I've
found someone!"

"Get them out then, Mangy Tail!"

The flowerpot was tipped over roughly and Rosa tumbled out. She scrambled to her feet, scared, dusty and dishevelled.

"Who are you?" the Sergeant demanded.

"N… no one!" Rosa stammered.

"I bet she's trying to help that silly princess, Sarge," said the mouse. "I bet she's a spy!"

The Sergeant nodded. "Take her to the dungeons!"

"No!" gasped Rosa. But Mangy Tail and another mouse took her by the arms. They were very strong and although she kicked and struggled they had no problem holding on to her.

"Stop your wriggling, Prisoner!" snarled

the Sergeant, poking her with the hilt of his sword.

Hastily Rosa did as she was told. She was dragged into the castle and through a big entrance hall before being pushed down a long flight of stairs. The Sergeant clambered round her and opened a heavy door ahead. "In there!" he ordered.

He pushed Rosa hard through the
doorway. She fell over and heard a bolt being
pushed firmly across the door on the other
side.

"You'll stay there until we tell King Rat
about you!" snapped the Sergeant through
the door. "Mangy Tail and Whiskers, you
guard her."

"Yes, Sarge!" said two eager voices.

Rosa's heart sank at the sound of heavy
feet traipsing away and the two guards
talking in low voices outside the door.

She shivered as she looked around her.
The room was very small with no windows.

Rosa bit her lip. How could she have been
silly enough to think she could get into the
castle so easily? She was trapped!

And what about King Rat? What would he do to her? And how would Nutmeg feel when she realised Rosa was missing? If the fairy had seen her being captured she would be so worried. Rosa felt awful. She had let her new friend down. There she'd gone again, just charging in without thinking.

I should never have headed off like that, she thought in despair. *I've just made it all worse.*

She looked at her shoes, hoping they might sparkle and whisk her away somewhere, but nothing happened. And Nutmeg couldn't rescue her by magic because she had told Rosa that her magic didn't work in the castle. *If I'm going to get out of here, I'm going to have to get myself out*, Rosa realised.

She thought hard. There were guards on the other side of the door but only two.

She went to the door and banged on it.

"Shut up!" snarled a mouse's voice from

the other side of the door.

"If you want food, there isn't any," said a
higher pitched voice.

Mangy Tail, thought Rosa recognising the
guard's voice from earlier.

"I don't want food," she said. "I don't feel
very well." She started to make sounds as if
she was about to be sick
as loud as she could.

"Yuck!" she heard
Whiskers exclaim. "If
she's sick in there I bet
we'll have to clear it up!"

"I just need some fresh air," said Rosa,
acting for all she was worth. "I'm sure I'll
be fine then but if I don't get some fresh
air I think I'll be sick EVERYWHERE!"

"Come on, come on, let her out," said Mangy Tail hurriedly.

Rosa heard the sound of the bolt sliding back and saw the door starting to open. She leaped to one side and crouched down in the shadows, staying as still as possible till the mice stepped into the doorway.

"Where are you?" Whiskers demanded, looking round.

Rosa leaped up, yelling as loudly as she could and the two mice jumped in alarm. Then Rosa charged at them, waving her hands about. It wasn't exactly a well-thought-out plan but hopefully it would do!

"Whoa!" Whiskers yelled, staggering into Mangy Tail and knocking him over. Rosa

leaped lightly over Mangy Tail's fallen
body, landing in perfect balance, before
pushing Whiskers with all her might. He
tripped over Mangy Tail, and they both
rolled into the room.

Rosa slammed the door shut and pushed
the bolt across, her fingers trembling. She'd
done it! She'd escaped!

The mice started banging on the door and shouting but it was a very thick door and the noise was muffled.

I'm free! Rosa thought. She raced up the stairs. No one was in the main hall. The front door was just opposite her. But just as she was about to make her escape, she saw the big door handle turn and heard a loud voice…

"So the prisoner's a girl, you say? A girl with red ballet shoes? But not the same girl who has been to Enchantia before?"

"A different one, King Rat. Definitely a different one."

Rosa ran through a nearby archway. There was a large chest and she ducked behind it.

"Take me to this prisoner then!" she heard King Rat snap.

Peeping out from behind the chest, Rosa
saw a black rat with a golden crown on his
head and a long purple cloak come marching
across the hall. He looked really scary with

his red eyes and
curling whiskers.
She hid back
behind the chest as
he headed for the
steps that led to the
room where she
had been kept
prisoner.

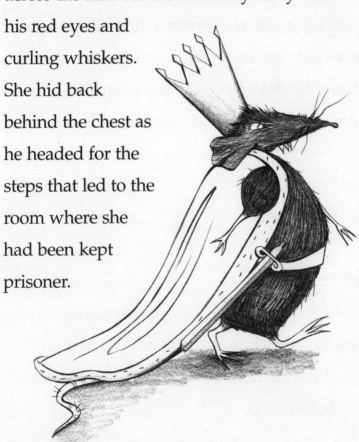

Oh no! As soon as he got there he would realise she had escaped!

She looked all around her. The chest was in a small corridor that seemed to be used for keeping bags of vegetables. Turning, she ran down it, her heart thudding. Any minute now, the guards would get out and come looking for her! What was she going to do?

Rosa's Plan

Rosa didn't know where she was going, but surely there must be a way out. She hurried down the corridor till she came to a small door in the wall. It looked like the door she had seen earlier from the outside of the castle. Her heart leaped. It was locked but there was a key in it!

She turned the lock and opened the door

and now she could see the woods just ahead of her! She ran towards them, faster than she had ever run in her life. With every stride she expected to hear voices shouting to stop and mice running after her but the only sound was of muffled yelling from inside the castle. She had a feeling her escape had just been discovered and the guards were in trouble but she didn't care. She had got out!

As she entered the woods, Nutmeg flew up to her. "Oh, Rosa! What happened?" The fairy looked scared stiff. "I saw the guards capture you. I didn't know what to do!"

"I'm really sorry," Rosa panted. "I was just trying to help the princess. I thought that if only I could get inside I might be able to hide and let her out tonight."

"It was really brave of you," Nutmeg said admiringly.

"It was really stupid," groaned Rosa. "I got locked in a room and I had to escape." She glanced around. "I think the guards might be after me at any moment."

"Quick, let's get out of here!" said Nutmeg. She grabbed Rosa's hand, waved her wand and spun in a pirouette. Silver and pink sparkles swirled around them and Rosa felt herself spinning round as Nutmeg's magic whisked them away.

They landed in a quiet clearing in the middle of the woods a safe distance away from the castle.

Rosa breathed out. "Phew!" She still had the key in her hand and her relief at escaping turned into excitement as she realised they now had a way to get into – and out of – the castle. She showed it to Nutmeg. "This opens the small door in the wall. We can use it to help Princess Cressida escape!" The fairy looked puzzled but a plan was already forming in Rosa's mind. "As soon as the princess comes back to her room, you can run up to the tower and sneak through the door. Then you and the princess can run downstairs and escape back out through the little door. If the guards come I'll distract them!"

"How?" asked Nutmeg.

"I don't know," Rosa admitted.

"Hmmm." Nutmeg started dancing to the

side, her feet crossing over quickly. Rosa recognised that it was a dance from *Swan Lake*. The fairy moved one way and then the other. "I always think better when I dance!" She spun round and then suddenly stopped, her eyes wide. "I know! I could use my magic to make you look exactly like the princess and teach you a dance she does! If the guards saw you dancing at the edge of the woods it would trick them and they'd run after you – leaving the coast clear." She frowned. "But it would be really dangerous for you."

"I don't mind!" Rosa said bravely.

"It might work. If you could just distract them for a few minutes, Cressida and I could run to the woods and then I could magic us all away," said Nutmeg.

"Let's do it!" said Rosa. She looked at the sky. The sun was just starting to set. They had to be quick. "Can you teach me the dance now?"

Nutmeg waved her wand and beautiful music from *Swan Lake* filled the clearing. "Copy me!" Nutmeg danced three steps forwards before turning three times, one arm above her head, one out to the side. Then she danced on in a big circle, turning with every step until she stopped in an arabesque, one leg held out behind her.

Rosa copied her. It felt wonderful to be dancing outside in the open air. She spun around letting the music flow through her. She didn't care if she got things a bit wrong; she just lost herself in the wonderful feeling. As she finished, she balanced on one leg.

Nutmeg looked very impressed. "You're really good at dancing, Rosa!"

Rosa smiled at her. "Thank you!" She felt even braver after the fairy's praise. "Do you think the mouse guards will have given up looking for me by now?"

"I should think so." Nutmeg nodded.

"Then let's go back to the castle!"

Nutmeg's magic took them to the edge of the forest... just as the sun was setting. The swan princess flapped her her wings and took off from the water.

Rosa watched the bird swoop into the tower.
A few minutes later, a girl in a white dress
appeared at the window. She had long
golden hair and looked sad.

"That's Cressida," said Nutmeg. "I'd better
make you look like her right away!"

Nutmeg began to dance around Rosa. A tingling started in Rosa's toes. It spread up her body and down her arms and up through her head. Nutmeg stopped and pointed her wand at her. There was a silver flash. Rosa blinked and gasped. Suddenly she was wearing a white dress. She put her hands to her head. She had a tiara on and her hair was now a deeper gold colour. "Oh, wow," she gasped. Nutmeg took a small mirror out of the pocket of her tutu and held it up. Rosa stared. Her own face wasn't looking back at her, but the face of the princess. It was a very weird feeling!

"How long will the magic last?" she asked quickly.

"Not long," said Nutmeg. "Some fairies in Enchantia can do transformation magic that lasts for hours but I'm still not very good at it. But it should last until Cressida and I escape." She rose into the air. "Good luck!"

"You too," called Rosa.

Nutmeg ran as fast as she could to the little door, and with one quick look back at Rosa, she disappeared inside.

Rosa took a deep breath. This was it! Nutmeg would hopefully be letting Princess Cressida out. *Oh, hurry up, hurry up*, she willed them. *Please get out before the guards come!*

"Hup two, hup two!"

It was too late. The guards were marching around the building. If Nutmeg and the princess opened the door now they'd be seen for sure!

Rosa didn't hesitate. Nutmeg and the princess were in danger. She had to help! Lifting her arms, she danced out of the trees…

Escape!

The two guards at the front of the group
stopped so that the guards behind bumped
into them. There was a chorus of "oofs" and
"ouches" as tails were trodden on and
swords tripped over.

"It's the princess!" the guards in the front
shouted as Rosa danced.

Rosa's heart somersaulted as the guards

started charging towards her. She turned and ran into the dark trees.

"STOP!" the guards yelled.

No way, thought Rosa as she ran in and out of the trees, jumping over tree roots and stumps. The ballet shoes seemed to help her, making her feet move more lightly than ever as she twisted and turned on the forest paths. She glanced behind her. The guards were getting closer!

But Cressida and Nutmeg were also running across the grass towards the trees, aiming for a spot far to the right. Luckily the guards were so busy chasing Rosa that they didn't look behind them. They raced after her.

Rosa headed in the direction that Nutmeg

and Cressida were going but as she did so, she realised there was a wall of trees and bushes in front of her. There was no way through. She was trapped!

"We've got her!" screeched Mangy Tail.

Rosa turned around as the guards skidded to a halt behind her. They formed a semi-circle, swords pointing at her. She backed up until she was pressed against the trees.

"Come on, Princess," snarled Whiskers through the dusk. "I don't know how you escaped but you're coming back to the castle with us right now before King Rat finds out…" He blinked. Rosa felt herself tingling all over and glanced down. The magic was wearing off!

"What… what's happening?" The guards began to back off in alarm as Rosa felt herself change.

Suddenly someone grabbed her hand from behind the tree.

"We're here!" Nutmeg's voice whispered.

Rosa's heart leaped.

"It's that girl!" said Mangy Tail suddenly.

Whiskers recovered from his confusion.

"It's a trick again! GET HER!" He and the

other guards leaped toward Rosa but at that very moment, Rosa felt Nutmeg's fingers tighten on hers.

"Hold on!" the fairy cried as a tinkling of music rang out.

And just as the guards' paws reached out to grab Rosa, a swirling curtain of silver and pink sparkles surrounded her and she felt herself being whisked away into the air, twirling round as if she was on a tea cup ride...

She landed a few seconds later. As the sparkles cleared, she realised that she was standing in a bedroom on a cream rug. Nutmeg was holding her right hand and Princess Cressida was holding her left.

"We... we escaped!" Rosa gasped.

"Only just," said Nutmeg, looking pale. "Oh, Rosa, that was so close!"

"Thank you so much for rescuing me!" Princess Cressida said, giving Rosa a hug as the bedroom door opened and a beautiful

lady in a blue dress with a golden crown
on her head looked in. "Oh my goodness!"
she cried, stopping in her tracks. "Cressida!
It's you!"

"Queen Isabella," said Nutmeg sinking
into a deep curtsey. Rosa quickly followed
her example.

Cressida however ran towards the Queen and hugged her. "I'm safe, Auntie! Rosa and Nutmeg rescued me! Oh, wait until you hear what happened!"

The Queen fetched the King and ten minutes later, Cressida and Nutmeg had told them everything. Rosa stood shyly at one side, not wanting to intrude. "Nutmeg used her magic to whisk us all back here," said Cressida, "and now we're safe!"

The Queen turned to Nutmeg and Rosa, grateful tears in her eyes. "Thank you, Nutmeg. And thank you, Rosa. You have both acted so bravely."

"I'm really glad I helped, but I did some

stupid things," admitted Rosa. "I should
never have gone off into the castle on my
own the first time. It could have turned out
really, really badly." She sighed. "My mum's
always saying I should think more before I
do and say things."

And she's right, Rosa thought, reminding
herself of Olivia.

The Queen smiled though.
"Do not be too hard on
yourself. It is good to act and
not just think, good to be
prepared to take risks,
good to be brave for the
sake of others. I think you
are a worthy owner of the
ballet shoes, Rosa." She

82

took her hands. "I am very, very glad you have been chosen to wear them."

"I am too," said Rosa happily. The adventure might have been scary but it had also been really good fun!

"You must not tell anyone about your time here," warned the Queen. "Keep the red shoes' magic secret."

"We should have a feast and dancing to celebrate Rosa's first visit to Enchantia," King Tristan declared. "Let the party begin!"

The rest of the evening passed in a whirl of eating delicious food, dancing to lively tunes and having fun. As they stopped after an energetic polka at midnight, Rosa felt her feet

tingling. At first she thought it was just because she had been dancing so much but then she realised that her shoes were glowing again. "I think I'm about to go home!" she gasped.

"Come back soon!" called Nutmeg. "Bye, Rosa!"

"Goodbye!" called Princess Cressida.

The last thing Rosa saw was Nutmeg and Cressida smiling and waving and then colours swirled around her and she was swept away...

Friends Again

Rosa looked around. She was back in the changing rooms!

She took a deep trembling breath. She could hardly believe everything that had just happened. No wonder Madame Za-Za and Delphie had told her the ballet shoes were special!

Glancing at the clock on the wall, she

saw that it was exactly the same time as when she had gone away. It was weird to think that no time had passed here while she had been doing so much. *And now she had something else to do*, she reminded herself. *I'm going to go home and ring Olivia and say sorry.*

Just as she finished getting dressed, she heard the main door of the ballet school open. There was the sound of running feet and then the changing-rooms door opened too. Olivia ran in. She stopped when she saw Rosa. "I forgot my cardigan," she said briefly. Grabbing it from the bench, she went to leave.

"Wait!" Rosa burst out. "Olivia, I'm sorry!" The words tumbled out of her. "I shouldn't have got cross earlier. I was just angry because I'd wanted to show you round. But it was stupid of me to lose my temper – I'm just too impetuous – and I really didn't mean to bump into you in class. It was just an accident. I am really, really sorry. Can we be friends again?" She held her breath.

But she needn't have worried. Olivia smiled almost instantly. "Of course we can."

Rosa felt a rush of relief.

"Do you want to come to mine for tea?" said Olivia. "We could stop at your house on the way and ask your mum if it's OK."

"Yes, please!" Even though Rosa knew she couldn't tell Olivia about Enchantia, she suddenly realised she could share her adventures with her in a different way. "There's this new dance I've learned. It's from *Swan Lake*. I could teach you it."

"That sounds cool," said Olivia. "Let's go!"

Rosa picked up her things. As she looked at the red ballet shoes she stopped and smiled to herself. *Thank you for the shoes, Delphie,* she thought.

She'd had an amazing time in Enchantia. When would she go again? And what would happen next time? Feeling excited, she put the shoes in her bag and ran after Olivia.

Tiptoe over the page to learn

a special dance step...

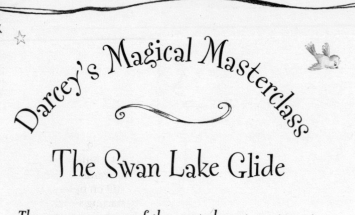

Darcey's Magical Masterclass

The Swan Lake Glide

The swans are some of the most elegant creatures in Enchantia. Try this running movement and see if you can be as elegant as they are and imagine your arms are like wings...

1.
Stand on your tiptoes with your arms held out to the side.

2.
Take little steps forwards whilst still on tiptoes, starting slowly and then move into a gentle, graceful run.

3.
Make your arms soft in the elbow and flap them gently up and down as if preparing for flight.

4.
Finish with a small jump into the air.

Magic Ballerina™
Rosa and the Golden Bird

The Wicked Fairy has captured the magical
Firebird and stopped any music playing in
Enchantia! Can Rosa help her friends to
dance once more?

**Read on for a sneak preview
of book eight…**

Rosa heard the sound of voices carrying through the still air. They were raised and angry. Through the trees, there was a small group of people. One of them was a slim fairy in a pale pink and brown tutu. Nutmeg!

Rosa's heart leaped at the sight of her friend. She began to run but as she got closer, she saw that the group were arguing with a large fairy wearing a black dress and a long cloak. Her grey hair was in a bun and she had a hooked nose and warts. She looked very scary. Rosa stopped at the edge of the clearing.

"Please let the Firebird go," one of the men in the group was pleading with her.

"No!" snapped the fairy.

"But you can't just keep him in a cage. It's mean and the birds in the forest need to be able to sing again!" said Nutmeg. "You have to release him!"

The fairy glared at her. "Have to! No one tells me I have to do anything. I will do exactly as I please!"

"No you won't!" cried Nutmeg. She stepped forward towards the fairy, hands on her hips. "We'll stop you!"

"Oh you will, will you? Well, we'll soon see about that!" There was a flash of light and a loud crack.

Rosa's hands flew to her mouth. The four people in front of the fairy were suddenly as still as statues. She had turned them all to stone!

Magic Ballerina

Darcey Bussell

Buy more great Magic Ballerina books direct from HarperCollins
at 10% off recommended retail price.
FREE postage and packing in the UK.

Delphie and the Magic Ballet Shoes	ISBN 978 0 00 728607 2
Delphie and the Magic Spell	ISBN 978 0 00 728608 9
Delphie and the Masked Ball	ISBN 978 0 00 728610 2
Delphie and the Glass Slippers	ISBN 978 0 00 728617 1
Delphie and the Fairy Godmother	ISBN 978 0 00 728611 9
Delphie and the Birthday Show	ISBN 978 0 00 728612 6
Rosa and the Secret Princess	ISBN 978 0 00 730029 7
Rosa and the Golden Bird	ISBN 978 0 00 730030 3
Rosa and the Magic Moonstone	ISBN 978 0 00 730031 0
Rosa and the Special Prize	ISBN 978 0 00 730032 7
Rosa and the Magic Dream	ISBN 978 0 00 730033 4
Rosa and the Three Wishes	ISBN 978 0 00 730034 1

All priced at £3.99

To purchase by Visa/Mastercard/Switch simply call
08707871724 or fax on **08707871725**

To pay by cheque, send a copy of this form with a cheque made payable to
'HarperCollins Publishers' to: Mail Order Dept. (Ref: BOB4),
HarperCollins Publishers, Westerhill Road, Bishopbriggs, G64 2QT,
making sure to include your full name, postal address and phone number.

From time to time HarperCollins may wish to use your personal data
to send you details of other HarperCollins publications and offers.
If you wish to receive information on other HarperCollins publications
and offers please tick this box ☐

Do not send cash or currency. Prices correct at time of press.
Prices and availability are subject to change without notice.
Delivery overseas and to Ireland incurs a £2 per book postage and packing charge.